James T. Franklin

Mid-Day Gleanings

A book for home and holiday reading

James T. Franklin

Mid-Day Gleanings
A book for home and holiday reading

ISBN/EAN: 9783337299491

Printed in Europe, USA, Canada, Australia, Japan

Cover: Foto ©Andreas Hilbeck / pixelio.de

More available books at **www.hansebooks.com**

Mid-Day

GLEANINGS.

————

A BOOK FOR HOME AND HOLIDAY

READING.

————

By JAS. T. FRANKLIN

————

MEMPHIS, TENN :
Tracy Printing and Stationery Co.
1893.

CONTENTS.

PROSE EDITION.

PREFACE

The contents of this book will doubtless be pleasing to its many readers, for its design is to suit the old as well as the young. Although the author is young, yet he may be mentioned as a self made gentleman of culture, and a natural born poet. When he was only seventeen he composed a beautiful piece of poetry titled "Rhyme on Home." This was the introduction of his poetic career. Since he has been distinguished not only as a lover, but as a composer of both prose and poetry.

His second poem, "The Wandering Heart," composed during an evening's walk, is said to have required only three minutes for its composition.

A few months after he graduated, which was in June, 1890, he composed this work. He is not confined to one talent, but possesses many, and, best of all, he has that hope in Christ, which he never forgets and walks according to his profession, which leaves a lasting Christian impression wherever he goes

Yours,

IDELLE ROBINSON.

INTRODUCTION

Although I do not claim any place among the poets and great authors of to-day, yet I present to the public what it has pleased me to prepare; and whether it is a worthy production, I leave it to the public to decide. This being the first effort of my life, and one which brings to me the pleasant memories of my school life and boyhood days, I ask the public to be not too hasty in condemning it. It is also well to say here, that the MID-DAY GLEANINGS will run through a series of volumes, which are now being prepared for the press. Each volume will contain a prose addition, which I hope will meet the hearty approval of all, as well as their just criticism.

THE AUTHOR.

MID-DAY GLEANINGS.

THE TRAIN OF LIFE.

Out from a lonely station,
    Bound for Greed and Gain,
A car went through creation
    Filled with people vain.

And over hills and valleys,
    And over the level plain,
Still rushing, crushing, pushing,
    Onward went the train.

Men of every station,
    In pleasure and pain,
Left off their occupation
    And boarded the train.

It stopped at every station
    Nothing was the fee—
Then hurried through creation
    Into eternity

THE EARTH AND MOON.

We wandered off from Father Sun,
    The silv'ry Moon and I :
A sep'rate kingdom we've begun,
    Out in the distant sky.

I dressed myself in green array,
    She dressed in silv'ry white ;
I kept the watch throughout the day,
    She watched throughout the night.

Although we claimed our royalty
    We feared our father's frown,
Until he, in his majesty,
    Presented us a crown.

It was a wreath of shining stars ;
    From nebulæ 'twas spun,
Suggested by my brother Mars,
    And polished by the sun.

Upon the moon he has bestowed
    His blessings long ago ;
To me he gave a veil of cloud,
    And handkerchief of snow.

A lightning arrow placed he here,
   A seven-colored bow,
That as we fly we need n. t fear,
   But triumph as we go.

Within our hands a little wand,
   Irresistible as air ;
We touch the meteoric strand
   And cause a shower there.

But arm in arm we keep our course,
   Just as it we ve begun :
Till soon we'll fly back to that source
   From whence we came—the sun.

LITTLE SUE.

IN MEMORY OF A DEAD FRIEND.

'Mong the stately larches, larches,
Where the willow arches, arches,
   And the lilies bow :
In the meadows yonder, yonder,
Little Sue would wander, wander,
   Looking for the cow.

Her brown eyes kept gazing, gazing,
Where some cows were grazing, grazing,
    'Mid the falling dew ;
And her voice kept calling, calling,
Though the dews were falling, falling,
    Soo cow ! Soo cow ! Soo !
Onward she went tripping,
Though the weeds were dripping
    With the early dew ;
'Til a little daisy
Asked, "Are you crazy,
    Pretty little Sue ?"
Then she hesitated,
As the truth she stated
    With a stately bow :
These my only troubles,
Wandering o'er the stubbles
    Looking for the cow.

Then under the larches, larches,
Where the willow arches, arches,
    And the lilies bow,
In the meadow yonder, yonder,
Onward she would wander, wander,
    Looking for the cow.
Her brown eyes kept gazing, gazing,

Where some cows were grazing, grazing,
　　'Mid the falling dew;
And her voice kept calling, calling,
Though the dews were falling, falling,
　　Soo cow! Soo cow! Soo!

She told unto the vine
That grew around the pine,
　　Of her mission true;
And the bramble nodded,
While onward she plodded,
　　The same little Sue,
When, only to plague her,
Forward sprang old ague,
　　And the fever, too;
Chased her to the dairy,
Smote her with malaria,
　　For wading the dew.
How her face did pallor,
As her cheeks grew sallow
　　With every breath;
Until a shroud was cut,
And her brown eyes were shut
　　By the hands of death.
And on the hilltop yonder, yonder,
Where she used to wander, wander,

'Mid the falling dew,
By the weeping willow, willow,
Under cowslips yellow, yellow,
    Lieth little Sue.
While under the larches, larches,
Where the willow arches, arches,
    And the lilies bow,
Homeward slowly plodding, plodding,
On the new grave trodding, trodding,
    Slowly comes the cow.

DREAM OF SCHOOL.

While sleeping at my window,
    In solemn hush of night,
I dreamed the sun above me
    Did give a brilliant light.

And bells were loudly ringing
    (Christmas now was o'er)
And voices gaily singing,
    At dear LeMoyne once more.

While children in the doorway,
    Preceptress on the stairs,
Professor in the office,

Were busied with affairs.

The teachers on the rostrum,
   And students, glad to meet
With music mistress smiling,
   Quietly kept their seat.

Accompanied by piano,
   Young ladies were singing
In alto and soprano,
   Their merry voices ringing.

Every heart elated,
   Intelligence in store,
An interest created,
   In their text-books once more.

The printing office open,
   Instructor in the door,
Was waiting for professor
   To send the classes o'er.

The students in the workshop
   Were busy with the saw ;
The manager, complaining,
   Was trying to find a flaw.

The day was gliding swiftly

And birds began to flock ;
The clock up in the steeple
    Had chimed out three o'clock.

And then I was awakened
    By fry of steak sirloin,
To find myself in Macon,
    Far from the dear LeMoyne.

JEFF DAVIS.

Ho, grim monster ! who art thou
    That hov'reth o'er my bed,
With bony form and wrinkled brow,
    Like a spirit of the dead ?
Back ! back ! stay thy bony hand !
    Come not near my bed.
I'm monarch of this Southern land,
    And fear not those from the dead.
" Hush !" said the monster, " hush,
    Let not an echo fly ;
Thy cheek must lose its healthy blush,
    For I am death—die ! "

Thou art death ? then challenge me ;
    Thou can'st not stop my mouth,

Not I, who quelled a raging sea
   And shook the Sunny South.
Then back! back ye goblin dim!
   Withstay your falling sword:
'Twas I who crushed a Southern whim
   And saved a Southern horde.
Then said the monster, "I know,
   So raise your voice and cry;
Call in both your friend and foe,
   For I am death—die'"

But wait, O death, consider fame,
   Regard immortal strife;
Behold what glory in a name,
   What happiness in life.
Consider, too, that civil strife.
   In which my fame was spread,
And how I conquered battlefields,
   And strew them o'er with dead.
Then said the monster, "No more!
   You cannot my sword defy;
Try not my mercy to implore,
   For I am death—die'"

But think ye of the war so long,
   I waged against the free,
In which I hurled a million strong,

Into vast eternity :
And how I sustained the battlefield
　'Gainst a dangerous foe,
And made the North almost to yield
　And let secession go.
There bravely fought I, man to man,
　Made Richmond's glory swell,
And wielded I the magic wand
　Until her glory fell.

Then said the monster, " That is true,
　But I do these defy ;
Naught else for you there is to do
　But think of death, and die."
Then fell the sword that rent apart
　The body from the soul ;
Then ceased the flutt'ring of the heart,
　For he had reached the goal.
His kinsman gathered to his side,
　The night-bird ceased its mirth ;
And friend and foe exclaimed, " He died
　An alien in the land of birth."

VOICE OF THE NATIONAL CEMETERY

O'er freedom's land, a happy dawn
  Disperses every cloud,
And o'er the victims, by victors drawn,
  Is the cold, bloody shroud;
And in thousands from the blood-washed
    field,
  And thousands from the sea,
Dropping the bayonet, sword and shield,
  Come plodding home to me;
While open throw I every door
  To satisfy their crave,
And I welcome all, both rich and poor,
  If they are of the brave.

Within my walls, 'mong cedars tall,
  'Mong flowers white and red,
Among the tombstones the shadows fall
  Quietly o'er the dead;
And the wandering clouds, in sunlight
    shrouds,
  O'erspread the soldiers' home,
While through my gateway great thronging
    crowds,
  At my swift bidding come;
But let them come, and here let them rest,

No trouble o'er them wave ;
For very soon they will be my guest,
  If they are of the brave.

A great Necropolis am I made,
  A palace for the brave,
With only a pickaxe and a spade,
  I am changed into a grave.
In corridor damp and mouldered cell,
  Lieth the honored head ;
And he who 'mong bravest warriors fell.
  Lies here among the dead.
E'en he who the Union flagstaff bore,
  When flags had ceased to wave,
Threw off the uniform that he wore
  And came to join the brave.

The bravest defenders of the right,
  The captains of the sea,
Who waged the battle and won the figh
  Are resting here with me.
Where funeral knells and tolling bell,
  And palace under ground,
In corridors damp and mouldered cells
  Their bodies there are found.
With pillows of stone, an earthen bed,

A sleep that nature gave,
A sheet of grass, and a flowered spread,
    Bid honor to the brave.

SOLITUDE.

'Mong lonely hills and silent dells,
    Where sunlight faintly gleams,
Without companion, nature dwells,
    And so beautiful she seems.

I love her, her plains most arid,
    For her home is solitude ;
To me a tongue speaks she varied
    And presents a scene most rude.

On the one hand is nature's plain
    And vastness of solitude ;
While on the other, hills serene
    Stand out in magnitude.

Behind me is the forest dark,
    Traversed by shadowy vale ;
And before me the brooklet---hark !
    How solemn is its tale.

The leaflets all, I know not why,

Happiness to me tender :
While far off in the bright blue sky,
  The sunbeams dance in splendor.

Through tree tops howl the savage wind
  'Mong branches leaps the squirrel :
In silence do the brooklets wend,
  And into an abyss hurl.

The golden rod and buttercup
  Perfume all the misty vale,
While little bees the honey sup
  And the rich perfume inhale.

The mocking bird sends up its trill,
  And loudly the owlet cries ;
From out the woods the whippoorwill
  In quivering notes replies.

While humming-birds and butterflies
  'Round the blooming red-bud tree,
And heaven with its blue arched skies,
  Are comfort enough for me.

A paradise are nature's wilds,
  Where the feet of man ne'er trod ;
Though Bacon says—"to like such wilds

You must be a beast or god."

But Bacon I do now defy,
  Let him be a lord or dude ;
For neither beast nor god am I,
  And I do love solitude.

I love the solitary waste,
  Where visits no form of beast ;
If God be there, and my heart chaste,
  Of fear I'd know not the least.

Joy I'd find in the wild recess,
  Encircled by insect lore ;
Never liking man the less,
  But solitude the more.

MY MOTHER'S GRAVE.

My mother died when I was young,
  Only nine months old, they say ;
And though I to my mother clung,
  They took her away from me,
And placed her in a lonely spot,
  The hill I have often seen,
And oft I've sought, but found her not,

Though the grasses still were green.
'Twas in the lovely month of May,
  The closing month of the spring;
And little birds in plumage gay
  Sad funeral songs did sing.
They watched the men with pick and sp
  So mournful did they wail;
But where that young mother was laid
  Little birds may tell the tale.
Though twenty years have passed since l
  And the birds are growing gray;
I've often asked of older men
  To tell me where she lay.

They answer thus—"I have forgot,
  But the grave I oft have seen,
'Tis on the hill, a lonely spot
  Where the grasses still are green."
But on the hill I searched in vain,
  And among the rustling leaves;
But ah! my heart is still in pain
  And my spirit often grieves.
Yet oft' I searched mid shine or rain,
  Though useless to me it seemed;
I often in her arms have lain
  And kissed her in my dreams.

And in my wake I ne'er forgot
  That dreaming alone I'd been,
But searched in vain that lonely spot
  Where the grasses still were green.

At last I saw a nice old jay
  Who could all but scarcely see;
His eyes were dim, his hair was gray,
  But he rose and bowed to me.
Oh birdie, will you tell me where
  My dear mother is, I pray?
And he asked me—"Was your mother fair,
  Or was she infirmed and gray?"

O, she was fair, yes, very fair,
  So young, and so pretty, too;
They buried her, I know not where,
  And I come to ask of you.
"Why, of course, I remember, lad,
  'Twas a lovely day in May,
They put your mother away, lad;
  'Twas just twenty years today

My family all have died since then,
  And I all alone am left;
They suffered all by wicked men,
  Who left me sad and bereft.
But beneath yonder great tree, lad,

'Neath that mossy covered mound,
Your mother there you will see, lad,
If there she can now be found,

For, lad, it is a lonely spot,
As lone as ever I've seen ;
But search and you will miss it not,
For the grass is tall and green."
I hurried beneath the giant oak,
Where its shady branches wave,
And there I saw a mound unbroke,
Which was my dear mother's grave.

I kneeled upon the lonely spot,
And thought the hill serene,
And wept because I found her not,
Though the grasses still were green.
But oft' I think she lies in state
While the stars are tapers tall ;
That by her side the angels wait
To see that no ills befall.

And whene'er ill becomes my lot
And death comes upon the scene,
I want to lie in just such spot,
Where the grass is tall and green.

"THE TIGERS AND THE KIDS."

High in the heavens rose the sun,
　　And tossed its beams about,
While I watched the children run
　　To see the throng turn out.

Where goes this throng, my bonnie lad ?
　　I asked a passer-by
Who in his hands a bat he had.
　　And now and then would cry—
"Hurrah for the 'Tigers,' boys'
　　And shame upon the Kids,
For, the Tigers sure were born, boys,
　　To beat the little Kids."

He stopped a moment, looked at me,
　　And fire flashed from his lids;
"The big boys are tigers, you see,
　　And the little boys are kids.
They are going to the picnic ground
　　To have a game, you see;
And if you want to take the round,
　　Come quickly, follow me,
And hurrah for the 'Tigers,' boys'
　　And shame upon the 'Kids,'

For never in history, boys,
    Were tigers beat by kids."

I joined in with the merry throng
    And boarded the Elmwood car,
And through the town we went along,
    And o'er the hills afar.
The people, they all stared at us
    And thought the world at end ;
Because it was a dreadful fuss
    That upward we did send.
But e'er and anon came the cry
    As fire flashed from their lids—
"The Tigers all deserve to die
    If they can't beat the Kids ;
Then hurrah for the 'Tigers,' boys,
    And shame upon the 'Kids ; '
There never was a hist'ry, boys,
    Of tigers beat' by kids. "

At last we reached the picnic ground,
    And Capt. Tiger wheeled
And placed the Tigers in the town
    And the Kids upon the field.
And then a ball was batted off
    That seemed to touch the sky ;

But down it came, by kid was caught,
  And hurrah went the cry—
"One tiger dropped out nicely, boys,
  And outed by the Kids;
Let every body shout, boys,
  For, they can't beat the Kids. "

And then a liner straight was sent
  Like lightning o'er the field,
Into a kiddish hand it went,
  Whose fingers would not yield.
" I have put another out, boys, "
  The kid did loudly cry,
" We sure will beat the Tigers, boys,
  Or we deserve to die. "
Another tiger turned about
  And batted off the ball;
When all the kids began to shout
  Before the ball could fall—
" He has put the whole side out, boys,
  That is just what he did;
And great Captain Tiger can't, boys,
  Beat little Captain Kid. "

Thus went the game for many hours
  Mid many a loud shout,

'Til the Kids said—"The game is ours,"
    And hurrah went the shout.
The game was called at 3 o'clock,
    The umpire said to us—
Dear friends it may your feelings shock,
    The game is standing thus:—
Forty-seven for Captain 'Kid,'
    For 'Tiger' twenty-seven,
And this is all the players did
    Since the clock struck eleven."

Then hurrahs shook the lofty air;
    The Kids, they grabbed the bat,
And left the Tigers standing there
    All quite chagrined at that.
But o'er the hills and back to town,
    Straight marched that mighty throng,
On every street that they went down
    They shouted out this song—
" Shame upon the Tigers, boys,
    And bully for the Kids,
For the Tigers are not born, boys,
    To beat the little Kids.
It was not in history, boys,
    The Tigers said this morn',
But hist'ry with this event, boys,

Its pages will adorn.
And shame upon the Tigers, boys,
  And bully for the Kids,
For Tigers were not born, boys,
  To beat the little Kids. "

AUTUMN

Autumn s Come !
  And he with his magic hands,
  By his polished easel stands,
With skill as great as renown,
Painting golden colors down.

Here he puts a touch of brown,
  Colors like his golden crown ;
Of the trees, in touches bold,
  Paints he ev'ry leaf in gold.

And the hilltops, far and near,
  In his picture stands out clear;
Over them a cloud floats by,
  And beyond the azure sky.

Here he paints a pretty vale,
  Overstrewn with lilies pale ;
While the silvery brooklet heaves,
  Spotted with the fallen leaves.

Then he leaves the shady bowers
   To paint the meadow and flowers,
And in amber paints the plain,
   Strewn over with golden grain.

Among his trees squirrels play,
   And birds flock in plumage gay,
While the orchards, very cute,
   All show up their golden fruit.

He paints, too, the old homestead,
   Where lived those who now are dead;
And in the meadows, children play,
   Running o'er the new cut hay

He paints the foundries and looms,
   The old church-yard and the tombs;
Vivid pictures of the brave,
   Paints he on the new made grave.

When his work is all quite done,
   He with canvas marches on
With the days bleak and dreary,
   Leaving souls weak and weary,
     Autumn's gone !

ECHOED THOUGHTS.

O darling will you let me tell
　　Just how I feel today;
How merrily chimes each Christmas bell,
　　As it echoes far away?

It makes me think of days gone by,
　　Of precious days well spent;
How Jesus left his throne on high,
　　On a godly mission bent.

The echoes of the distant bells
　　Strange fancies bring to me,
Like flowers in a lonely dell,
　　Your own sweet face I see.

And when comes even' on at last,
　　And frost has chilled the air,
I think again of days gone past
　　And bless thee in my prayer

O, if you could only think
　　Of whom I dream in sleep;
Could you but dream as fairies dream,
　　You'd know the secret I keep.

Could you but guess, and that you can't,
　　Though you may dream and weep;

This secret in my heart I plant
  A thousand fathoms deep.

I dream of thee, I dream of home,
  So sweet can memories be ;
I visit where I once did roam,
  I dream of eternity.

IDA BELLE.

'Twas of thee, fair woman, with sad, sweet
    face,
  • That the poets dreamed of old ;
'Twas the mirrored expressions of thy face
  That sculptors tried to mold.

To live in thy charms the lover has sighed
  Until his cheeks were paled,
And it was thy picture which artists tried
  To paint so oft' and failed.

Sweetest perfection itself thou art,
  Thy face is a poet's dream,
And through the eye, the window of thy
    heart,
  Both love and kindness beam.

And thy very sad song, which gives you
    fame,
  Would bring angels from above ;
A single smile from your lips would inflame
  A human heart with love.

For you, like the dazzling sunbeams go,
  To light this mundane sphere ;
To scatter rich blessings, instead of woe,
  Make earth ten-folds more dear.

Like the trailing of the comet bright
  That spans the canopy ;
Trail on forever thy arcs of light,
  Let man thy beauty see.

Thou art a queen, whom heaven has blessed,
  Thy throne morality ;
Thy palace with truthfulness is dressed,
  Thy crown is purity.

O woman, so noble, so pure, so proud,
  Sit fast on virtue's throne,
Till eternity round thee casts her shroud
  And bears thee to thy home.

CORRUPTED MINISTRY

O corrupted ministry!
 How long can you endure
In foulest iniquity,
 Pretending to be pure?
Our churches have you blacken'd
 With your darkest deeds of shame,
Disgraces have you spreaded
 O'er the fairest woman's name.
The churches have been auction'd
 At a price below their cost,
The Devil was the bidder;
 O, God! will the church be lost?

Our preacher is a drunkard,
 And the deacon will be soon;
The church is a fighting ring
 And the pulpit a spittoon.
Ordaining is a mockery,
 For the elder is a farce,
His interest all is lacking,
 And morality is scarce.
With cigar and the bottle
 In Jehovah's holy name,
He goes among our women
 To scatter seeds of shame.

The husband he has parted
  From the most beloved wife,
Humiliates the mother
  And wrecks the daughter's life.
The peaceful homes are broken,
  The seeds of strife are sown,
The parson takes some man's wife
  And forgets about his own.
On Sunday morn he preaches—
  "Walk the commandments in,"
Meanwhile his soul is blushing,
  And his heart is black with sin.

Newspapers on the altars
  Leave a terrifying stain,
While the preacher stands and sells
  And keeps the ill-gotten gain.
The preachers, they are lodgemen,
  And the bishop, he is, too,
And so cannot chastise them,
  No matter what sin they do
The secret lodge is cursing
  Great Jehovah's holy name,
And does a deadly mission
  In secret and in shame.

O how long must we endure

This great sin to take its course?
If we would the church secure,
　　We must break sin down by force.
All the pulpits need be cleansed,
　　And the churches to be scoured,
The shrine of purity restored
　　Where once the Christians bowed.
Some volunteers are wanted
　　Whose hands will ne'er grow cold,
No drunkards ever needed
　　In the Christian's sober fold.
No man is a gentleman
　　And no preacher a divine
Who smokes cigars, drinks, or chews,
　　Or mingles with the wine.

THE CLOT OF BLOOD.

In thought I stood on Nashville bridge,
　　Just over the vast expanse,
Where Cumberland rolls her turbid stream
　　And the merry ripples dance.

The sunlight sparkled on the bridge
　　And o'er the balustrade.
I stepped out upon the edge
　　To list' what the waters said.

I bent my ear—and low the sound
   Of groans, the waves among—
I stood and list' until I found
   'Twas there a man was hung.

"O stranger," sang the waters dark,
   " Look on the balustrade,
Where crime has left his bloody mark,
   Though the victim be dead."

I bent my eyes, and lo! I saw
   A clot of human blood
That told me of a savage law
   Where crime for justice stood.

O waters, tell me all, I cried,
   Lay bare the human heart ;
"The crime was dark," the waters sighed,
   "Unfitted to impart."

"But stranger, list'," the waters said,
   " For God has made it so,
The deeds of man, though he be dead,
   Should here forever show.

Bad deeds are like the clot of blood,
   So dark beneath the sun ;

The rain, it came ; the blood, it stood,
  To show a crime was done.

So let your deeds be always good,
  Light-houses 'long the shore ;
The storm, it came : the light-house stood,
  Its lights shone all the more.

O stand ye firmly for the right !
  'Tis all we have to tell ;
Now we must hasten in our flight,
  Oh stranger, fare the well !"

"*MATTIE.*"

O woman, in thy loveliness,
  In grace and truth combined,
Made so perfect by thy pureness,
  Made famous by thy mind ;
'Neath the heaven's dazzling sunlight,
  Thou art a sparkling gem ;
Thy deeds, like stars, are shining bright,
  For God has polished them.

Should I but say as others say,
  True sweet saying of old,

That your value, if you would weigh,
  Would be your weight in gold ;
Then think you would my sayings false,
  Not meant for you at all ;
A piece of gold exact your weight
  Would be a deal too small.

A million times your weight in gold,
  Rubies of every kind
Could never, if the truth was told,
  Outbalance your great mind.
A head so small, a brain so great,
  Wonderfully contrast ;
Think not young woman of thy weight,
  But hold thy knowledge fast.

Few like you have attained so much,
  And few like you so small ;
But from the height that you have reached
  Be sure and never fall.
There in this wide world of ours
  A mission is for you ;
Help others rise, help others live,
  Do all that you can do.

Know ye it is the noble soul,
  In a cold world like this,

That rises upward from the goal
    Unto the hight of bliss?
Then noble be your words and deed,
    Let wisdom be your guide,
For wisdom's path to glory leads,
    The gate is standing wide.

GROVER CLEVELAND.

Hurrah for Cleveland! the nations cry,
As their exultation shakes the sky
And Grover rises upon high;
While through his piercing eyes looks down,
Watching oceans as they frown;
He seeth the dark and threat'ning cloud,
And heareth the peals of thunder loud,
And yet feeleth he himself so proud,
He sallies still more high.

America justly needs be proud,
For rich and poor have before him bowed,
And he smiled o'er all the crowd;
But, in turning he himself around,
Having heard a muffled sound,
While studying the faces o'er,
And a helping hand he gives to poor,

He leaves a note at every door—
"Your rights in me are found."
He will show what "justice and law " is,
While old England raiseth up her voice
And claims she must rejoice
That, in Grover Cleveland, now is found
Hopes for the world around ;
That some gratitude the nations owe,
And favor certainly will they show,
While in free trade ships they come and go,
And never cause a wound.

The stars and stripes will the nations praise,
And many a cheer for Cleveland be raised
While at the White House he stays ;
For strike he will the much-needed blow,
Make abundant money flow,
And the money he will circulate
Through every home, in every State,
And our joys will he accelerate
And set our hearts aglow.

O, thou eagle: in thy scope so wide,
Go higher still, for no ills betide,
While thou, the nation's pride,
Unfurls the banner o'er our head,
That bears this motto : " Bread !"

Flags of Democracy, o'er the brave,
From the mountains to the sea shall wave,
And voices rise up from the grave —
" 'Tis well, no more be said."

JEALOUSY 'MONG THE FLOWERS

A flower garden seemingly
    Was this whole world of ours,
And through this garden dreamingly
    I wandered mong the flowers.

And I saw flowers gayly dressed,
    Some in form of women fair,
And some, as I have since confessed,
    Had a dark or auburn hair.

Some personated mignonette,
    And some like the daisy fair,
While lovely little violets
    Kissed me everywhere.

Among so many flowers fair
    I saw a blushing little rose,
While by her side the lilly fair
    So quietly did repose.

I touched the lilly as I said
    A kiss must be my fee,
But her cheeks turned a crimson red—
    She turned away from me.

But that, I said, will never do
    For lilly so sweet and fair,
For it has been said, and 'tis true,
    "Lil is fairest of the fair."

So then she turned the pouting lips
    Upward to receive the kiss,
But no! no! cried jealous cow-slip,
    Not in this garden of bliss.

And then I asked her if she would
    When we together strolled.
No plotting here! that's understood,
    Chimed in Miss Marigold.

Then Love with "Lil" I tried to plight,
    With vows quite old in story,
But, ah, you know that is not right,
    Chimed in Miss Morning Glory

Then all the flowers cried at once,
    His love will never be true,

"So 'Lil' ought to give him the bounce—
    That's just what I would do."

" Ugly imp," said a dry old maid,
  " He ought to have said it to me,
And he would see I'm not afraid
    To show what a woman should be."

" Hush! hush!" said the little Snow-drops,
  " Your words are so needless said;
Old maids this year are sorry crops,
    Therefore be thou not afraid."

" I second that," said wee Fox-glove,
  " For grandpa has often said
That man was a fool to ever love
    An out o' fashion old maid."

" It is true his love is not pure,"
    Said jealous Forget-me-not;
" His taste is bad, and that is sure,"
    Said the frisky Touch-me-not.

" Well, I am fairest of you all,
    And I have received no kiss,
Not even one," said Miss Snow-ball,
    "And I'm quite vexed at this."

" Well, let us see," said old Lark-spur,
 " I'll tell you what we'll do,
We'll tell a lie on him to her,
 And we'll cut their love in two."

" I'll tell the lie," said Devil-weed ;
 " I'll stir up all the strife,
I'll start up such a lie indeed
 She'll hate him all of her life."

And then like lightning sped he on
 His mission so foul and wrong,
'Till even the Dandelion
 Was deceived by his tongue.

And thus to Lily he began :
 " With him your love must now end—
A disguised snake is that man
 Who claims to be your friend.

I swear it that he, this same day,
 Some big lie has told on you,
That people all who hear it say
 ' I wonder if it is true.' "

Then Lily turned her back on me
 For what that tattler said,

And all the flowers said to me:
    "Your character has been read,

So out of here yourself you take."
        Said all the flowers, "Begone!"
Then suddenly did I awake
        To find myself alone.

MUD.

Ah, my soul, what wet and dreary days,
And how I crave the sun's bright rays,
For down this never ending lane,
Plodding daily through the rain,
Brings from my heart a heavy thud—
My eyes behold nothing but mud,
        Nothing but mud.

But every morning mid the poor
From my home to the schoolhouse door,
Splashing through the supple clay,
Toiling wearily on my way,
Makes my heart keep up the thud
While before me nothing but mud,
        Nothing but mud.

Mud on the door-step, mud in the door,

Mud on the ceiling, mud on the floor,
Mud outside, and mud in the road
Mud on the gateway and abroad ;
Mud at table, and mud in bed.
And mud o'er great creation spread ;
While this lonely, thumping thud,
Makes me think that man is mud,
   Nothing but mud.

But, ah, my soul, why not content,
Complaint to grief always gives vent,
And the more exalted thou be,
The greater seems the fall to thee,
So, weary heart, forget thy thud,
Be content, though the world be mud,
   Nothing but mud.

THE MODEL QUEEN

TO IDELLE.

Thou wert not born in a palace,
 Nor hath thou worn the regal crown ;
Or the diamond-decked apparel
 Like the stately belle of the town.

But lived, thou hast, a lady,

Both at home or when abroad;
And that is a priceless treasure,
   Worth diamonds by the load.

Thy fingers decked, were not with rings,
   But youthful hands to work were trained;
Not were holidays in leisure,
   But were in studies hard retained.

An adept now in thy studies,
   And to manual labor prone;
An heiress to every virtue,
   Is a lot that is all thy own.

Thou didst not pine for a title;
   Thy wants thou didst ever control;
Although thou hadst a woman's pride,
   A woman's heart, a woman's soul.

Like the queen who, as milkmaid dressed,
   But whose hands spoke true to the wise;
Virtue shows the noble being,
   Though you be under disguise.

No royal suitor yet has come,
   At thy feet to kneel and to plead;
Yet thousands of worshipful hearts
   Regard thee a treasure indeed.

Thou art a princess, yea, a queen,
  The proud possessor of wealth;
For virtue to thy cheeks gives bloom,
  And to thy soul eternal health.

That thou shalt have a higher sphere,
  Is the noble decree of fate;
That thou wert crowned by royal hands
  Will be known at the Golden Gate.

Though snares on every hand beset,
  Wherever thy feet hath trod;
An angel crowned with honors yet
  You'll dwell in the palace of God.

QUEEN OF THE FLOWERS.

When wandering through the fields one day,
  And through the meadow coming,
I found a flower on my way,
  It was a lily blooming.

Up from the flowers all around
  She raised her stately form,
And then, if e'er before, I found
  A solace within a charm.

She was kissed by the morning sun,
   Though the sunbeams made her blush;
Her happy life had just begun,
   So warbled out the thrush.

Up from her stalk a sweet perfume
   That spread the meadow over,
And kissed the flowers all in bloom,
   E'en to the meadow clover.

Made many flowers raise their heads
   And call modest lily sweet,
While others from their humble beds
   Walked out to kiss her feet.

And every worm and shrub and tree,
   Even the Apple green,
Unanimously did agree
   To call her the " flower queen. "

And then the lark and linnet came
   Singing loud—" May honor show
That well may fare the lily's name,
   And in beauty may she grow. "

A coronation song they sang,
   And the chorus joins and sings;

Through all the meadow music rang,
   Like harps of a thousand strings.

The band of music was the bee;
   The jay bird acted soldier;
He wore a cap upon his head,
   And stripes across his shoulder

Soprano sang the mocking bird
   'Til the tenor took its place;
Alto sang all the sparrow hawks,
   And the bullfrog sang the base.

While thus presented they the crown
   A spectator old and gray
Came forward in his royal gown
   And he thus began to say—

" Fairest queen of all the flowers '
   Thy lips are a sacred thing,
Though many bees may buzz about,
   Beware ! they have a sting.

Be not deceived by bees and bugs
   Who praise those lips of thine,
For soon they'll stoop to ask a kiss,
   And then you must decline.

Or else you will attraction lose,
    Thy fragrance and thy charm ;
For every bee who takes a kiss
    Will take away thy balm. "

DON'T KISS.

TO THE GIRLS.

Beware, sweet girl, and do not kiss,
    Place not your honor at stake ;
When hear ye the serpent's hiss,
    Look close, you will find the snake.

The serpent comes in every kiss,
    If dressed in masculine guise,
And always shows without amiss
    That virtue it does despise.

Sometimes the dudes at close of eve,
    Reposing at your gate,
Wish for a kiss before they leave ;
    Beware ! it seals your fate.

For kissing, like the tiger's thirst,
    When tasted human blood ;

One victim caught is not the worst
  That's to be understood.

But others seeks, and in the end
  The modest and the true,
Without warning from a friend
  Is made a victim, too.

Beware, too, of your lover's lips
  When they're caressing yours,
For next his arm steals 'round the waist
  He seemingly adores.

You think him harmless as the doves,
  Poor girl, be not deceived '
Not ev'ry man who says he loves
  Can always be believed.

The serpent's kiss has many forms,
  And heeds no laws of right.
He has the most bewitching charms
  And prowls around at night.

Sometimes it is the married man
  Who claims he has the right,
Because he is your mother's friend,
  To kiss you a good night.

Beware ! he is the adder bold
   That never spares his prey ;
So if you would your virtue hold,
   Be warned and flee away.

Sometimes at parties, too, you'll find
   Young men who want to kiss,
But ah ! the serpent lurks behind
   The thought that wishes this.

Again beware ; be true to trust ;
   Always remember this :
Whatever lad tells you you must
   Tell him you do not kiss.

WAYSIDE CREAM.

'Twas mirth and titter the day live-long,
   'Twas fun at any cost,
'Twas joy mingled with music and song,
   And jests of the merry host.

The brilliant sun from his western throne
   Shot forward his arrows bright,
And fairy-like on the carpet down
   Fell the brilliant arcs of light.

A merry group was gathered round
   To welcome a sweet brunette;
And dishes made a clattering sound,
   While tables for dinner were set.

"Come in, ladies," the hostess said,
   "And gentlemen, come in, too;
'Tis dinner time, and the feast is spread,
   I prepared it all for you."

To head of the table went Miss Key,
   And I to the side did get;
Before me was the beautiful Belle,
   At her side the sweet brunette.

Who has ordered cream? said I to "Lu,"
   It was sister, answered she;
"No! No!" said Belle, as if it were true,
   "I think it was Miss Key."

However, to us came not the cream,
   And there were many sighs;
Miss Belle was like a beautiful dream,
   As the tears welled to her eyes.

Then to me she whispered in a moan,
   "If we should perchance to meet

The messenger who for cream has gone,
   We will stop him on the street.

So in my pocket she hid a spoon,
   And we went our journey on ;
But alas! came the fun too soon,
   Ere we had our journey done.

For with the lovely little brunette
   I had tripped across the dell;
She at my side is smiling yet,
   Around me she casts a spell.

When suddenly from the dell below
   There arose a startling scream ;
And back the ladies started to go,
   For some one was bringing cream.

Yell after yell, from beautiful Belle,
   Quite threw me into a swoon ;
She threw off from me the lovely spell,
   And searched me for the spoon.

And with spoon in hand she made a rush
   Toward him who bore the cream ;
Brunette's face took a rosy flush,
   So full of joy did she seem.

Her sister, though, so happy she was,
   Her face was no longer a dream ;

Reality on her countenance was,
   As she made way with the cream.

A party, happy, were we and gay,
   But a few things I'll never forget ;
The most thrilling pleasures of that day,
   And the face of the sweet brunette.

But in the height of our joy we feared
   That danger would happen soon;
For all of the cream had disappeared,
   And with it went the spoon.

SONG OF THE SLAVE.

Oh, send me home to Africa,
   Back across the sea,
From America's cruel shores
   To my own country.
For there my heart is yearning,
   Where the Southern sun is burning :
Oh, could I but be returning
   To the home of the free.

Oh, how I long for Africa,
   Home of Liberty,
Where happiness forever dwells

And all men are free.
It is there I should be going,
   Where the bread-fruit trees are growing,
And sweet freedom s breeze is blowing ;
   ' Tis my own country.

Oh, send me home to Africa,
   O'er the raging sea,
To the Lake Tanganyika,
   In my own country.
Where the children all are singing,
   And in hammocks they are swinging,
While sweet freedom s song is ringing
   In the land of the free.

Oh, send me home to Africa,
   Where I long to be,   ·
From this cruel America
   O'er the raging sea,
Where my fathers all are reigning
   And their freedom still retaining ;
O, they never are complaining
   In that land of the free.

Oh, send me home to Africa,
   Home across the sea,
Where happiness forever dwells,

And all men are free.
'Tis for there I still am sighing
  If, perchance, I should be dying
Upward I would go a flying
 From my own country.

THE LAST SNOW

Fall on, ye fairy snowflakes,
  Scatter over the town;
'Tis night, but when the day breaks,
  You'll sparkle on the ground.

For winter from his palace
  Has just begun to move,
And shakes ye fairy snowflakes
  O'er temple, hill and grove.

With gleaming eyes he watches
  The snowflake as it falls,
And then, with icy fingers,
  He paints the temple walls.

O'er all the earth he breathes
  A cold and bitter breath;
The dripping water freezes,
  And things are still as death.

With cold and icy fingers
   He shrouds the earth in snow ;
His fingers touch the brooklets,
   And waters cease to flow.

Grim winter is an artist
   Surpassing man in skill;
In white alone he pictures
   The valley, grove and hill.

His trees are white and drooping,
   Laden with the snow ;
A freezing breath he breathes,
   And wondrous beauties show.

O, man, could you but picture
   Humanity in white ;
Make every deed conspicuous
   In snowy colors bright,

This earth would be a heaven—
   A world of wondrous bliss--
Where blessings would be given,
   And love and mercy kiss.

"OTTO."

From rock city in highland rim,
Where seldom azure skies grow dim,
From Meharry's Medical Hall,
To sunny bluffs where shadows fall,
To our city like templed Rome,
We welcome Dr. Otto home.

A course in school he did begin,
And year went out as year came in,
And still did he a course pursue ;
One object kept he still in view,
Till he had found just what he sought,
In life's battle he stood and fought.

And when the battle was achieved,
He did not dare to stand aggrieved,
But he, rejoicing, homeward bent,
His heart was full, his mind content,
Now that he could help all mankind,
No suff'ring soul he d leave behind.

A happy life is his indeed,
For happiness does man most need ;
Success, it seems, does come to earth,
And to new life does she give birth,

For a new life has he begun,
A battle fought, a victory won.

Then may he reach the height of fame,
No wrong e'er blot his titled name.
His name on hearts, where'er he goes,
He writes in love, and there it grows,
For courage in the battle strife
Has wrought this change in Otto's life.

BRIDE OF THE SKIES.

With the gentle zephyr of a summer's twi-
    light,
When heard, a single sound was not,
Save, being rustled by the gentle winds, the
    leaves
And zephyr's almost silent, footfalls
Came—a voice that, in heavenly sweetness,
    said :
" Behold her beauty, Bride of the Skies !"

Then came the silent zephyr, in her fairy
    form,
Stooping, my burning cheeks she kisses,
While my aching brow with airy palm she
    fans.

Thrilling my soul by gentle touches,
She catches me up in her gentle arms
And bears me into the chamber of the
    bride.

And there the moon, great mirror of heaven,
    before,
Stood dressed the fair and lovely comet,
Surpassingly beautiful as she twists and
    turns,
And smiling, her lovely form surveys,
While in her chamber a million candles
    swung,
Without the guests to the wedding come.

But stands she stately and proud in the pal-
    ace hall,
And about her gathers her snow white
    robes,
When the proud but invisible Eternus comes,
And, entering her bridal room,
Takes her, and upon his breast her head
    she pillows,
While kisses upon her lips he rains.

Then upon his knees falleth the Prince
    Eternus,

And a ring, with sparkling meteors set,
Draws he from his invisible bosom,
And, while her hand he clasps and presses,
As she, blushing and smiling, kneeleth be-
    side him,
He places it upon her finger.

Rising, with a diadem of stars he crowns
    her,
When graceful Venus, her bridesmaid,
    comes,
And with airy touches from her graceful
    fingers,
That electrify the blushing bride,
Catches she up, of flaming light, a snowy
    veil,
And spreads it over the bridal robes.

Then softly from earth to heaven is raised
Music, the sweetest by man e'er heard,
And into the blazing skies earth and sea
    looks up,
When the soft, low wedding march begins,
And planets swing in their beautiful orbs
    and nod,
While time to music they try to keep.

O, that an angel might paint that scene so
    sublime '
Describe that proud procession of stars,
For slowly caught up by the moon and re-
flected,
Seems the whole heaven ablaze with light,
While everywhere the feet of the bride doth
    tread,
'Neath them skyrockets burst forth and
    blaze.

Through the heavens her graceful form she
    carries,
And her robe of light serenely trails,
Until her last glance at the mirror she
    snatches,
Then, moving slowly from the zenith,
Takes her seat upon the western horizon,
While floats her trail in the eastern sky

A WANDERING HEART

A little heart once wandered out
    To see what it could see :
It raised its voice in gladsome shout,
    Rejoiced that it was free.

It laughed and wept, sighed and slept,
   And dreamed of future fair,
That fairies to its side had crept
   While it was sleeping there.

It then awoke with gladsome smile
   And turned it round about,
But fairies fled into exile,
   And not a one was out.

Again it shook its haughty form
   And started on apace,
Then paused to give a greeting warm
   To a little flower vase.

Then off it leaped with sudden bound,
   O'er the flowery spray,
Over the rocks and mossy mound,
   It plodded on its way

It heard the little cricket's song,
   The birds, it heard them, too;
Beside the river it walked along
   Well bathed in the morning's dew.

It rushed into the lonely dell
   Where mortals never roam,

But there it found no place to dwell,
    There was no place like home.

So on it went the world around,
    With no one would it join
'Til it came to Memphis town
    And entered in LeMoyne.

And there for once it ceased to roam,
    (Poor thing, it needed rest),
And tried to find a better home,
    Within another's breast.

" But ah! sad heart, a foolish choice
    To make thyself a slave, "
Was heard to say a spirit's voice,
    " 'Tis better in the grave. "

Thus refused a resting place,
    It wept and onward went :
With care it studies every face
    While on love's mission bent.

THE NIGHTINGALE OF SONG.

TO "SIS."

One Summer's night in month of June,
At half-past eight, or not as soon,
I sat enraptured in my seat
List'ning to strains unearthly sweet.

They came like the summer's shower,
Refreshing every bush and bower,
Drifting on the still night air,
Falling freely, purely and rare.

They came from lips of a dark brunette,
With eyes as dark as midnight jet;
Her face was sad, her form was neat,
Her lips, no doubt, unearthly sweet.

She sang a song in smooth accent,
That made my heart to joy give vent;
And my very soul exalted rose
Beyond the sky to quiet repose.

I wandered off in heav'nly lands,
Through verdant fields, on golden strands;
I thought I heard an angel sing,
" Love, I'll hide thee under my wing."

And then I heard the echoes swell,
Sounding o'er earth in ev'ry dell;
Then lifted up by balmy breeze,
Were wafted far beyond the trees.

Again the echoes rose on high,
And drifted far beyond the sky;
My soul rose up on wings of bliss,
My heart went out to receive a kiss.

When the singer's song had ended,
My soul again to earth descended;
I found myself in a chapel grand,
In a city of my native land.

I sat there with my eyes transfixed;
My thoughts were gone, my brains all mixed;
I tried if I one smile could gain
Ere the singer had ended her strain.

But not a one could I engage;
She heeded me not, and left the stage;
But when the people gave applause,
She was called again: without pause

She rose and sang it o'er again,
The same sweet song, the same sweet strain;
And, wandering on the same old route,
With the singer's song my heart went out.

And sometimes now, in accents clear,
That same sweet voice falls on my ear;
Those same bright eyes, that same sweet
    face,
Smile upon me in ev'ry place;
And ever now, as life glides on,
Upon my soul sweet visions dawn.

CHRIST'S WHISPER.

When my heart grew weak and weary,
And the days grew bleak and dreary,
I heard a voice so gently calling,
Upon my ears softly falling—
" Come, even while sea billows roar,
Unto this fair but unknown shore. "

That same voice still is calling me—
" Come, come away across the sea;
Come while the tide does ebb and flow,
And the winds do softly blow;
Come even while sea billows roar,
Unto this fair but unknown shore.

Softly still it is calling me,
Merrily calling, full of glee,

Borne on the night winds o er the sea,
Floating gently o'er the lea,
Calling as sweetly as before—
" Come to this fair but unknown shore. "

Somebody still is calling me—
" Come over the deep and dark blue sea ;
Come in the morn or dewy eves,
Haste thou on ere my spirit grieves ;
For I am waiting as before
To give thee welcome on this shore. "

And yet that voice is calling me,
Merrily calling, full of glee.
Borne on the night winds o'er the sea,
Floating gently over the lea,
Falling sweeter than before—
" Oh, come ' come to this unknown shore. "

Then merrily, merrily go,
While the winds do softly blow,
Oh merrily, merrily go,
While the tide does ebb and flow.
And even while sea billows roar
Go view that fair and unknown shore.

THE VALENTINE.

A little maple once was I,
  A reed of flax were you,
Within a meadow, side by side,
  We both together grew.

A happy life we both did lead,
  And great in nature grew;
A lovely pair we were, indeed,
  And made a lovely view.

We might have together grown,
  A maple and a flax,
Had the wicked farmer mercy shown,
  And spared us from his ax.

Off to the manufactory
  He took you far away,
While to the hungry old saw-mill
  He carried me next day.

They wove you into snow-white cloth,
  A cloth of linen kind,
And scooped me out into a tray,
  As thin as thinnest rind.

First into paper, then to board,

They pressed you nicely down,
While butter in my scooped out tray,
  They sent around the town.

You were bought by a nice young man,
  And I by a lady fair,
And then our last career began,
  And here s the whole affair :

They were courting, or they feign
  A lover s bond to form ;
She paints me 'til a lovely scene,
  He takes me under his arm.

A plug he cuts from out your back,
  Then with some ribbon red,
And with some blue and green, intact,
  He binds me there instead.

So, after many years we meet,
  Though once in verdure fine ;
We now are pleased the world to greet,
  As some one's valentine.

DISAPPOINTMENT.

"'Tis Easter, Tom," says Legs to me,
    "And you just bet your worth
If I'm there at half-past three
    I am biggest man on earth.

I want you just to come and go,
    No better you'd deserve
Than see me kiss that pretty girl
    Who lives beyond the curve.

Come, take the car, I'll pay your fare,
    And haste, I prithee,
For she expects me to be there
    Just as the clock strikes three."

So, with collar up to his chin,
    He took the red street car,
And later on we both walked in
    Where gates did stand ajar.

He rang the bell, then gave a grin,
    And seemed as lost in bliss;
He was sure she would let him in
    And he would steal a kiss.

Some footsteps sounded in the hall;

He made ready to embrace,
For I am sure I saw it all
Written upon his face.

" Magnetta, ope the door," he said,
And soon it came ajar.
But there before us, in her stead,
Stood Magnetta's pa,

Who calmly smiled at us, and said:
"Gentlemen, walk straight in."
Legs, blushing, turned a crimson red,
And lost that pleasant grin.

But there we stayed three hours or more,
Yet no girl did we see.
At length I said, " Legs, let's go,
The engagement was at three."

We took our leave, that Easter day,
When Legs did some one see,
Down the road he darted away—
"Come, Tom, this is she."

I can not tell you how it was,
But this is what I saw :
He did not kiss her, as he thought,
Because it was her ma!

No girl we saw the live-long day;
 'Twas very strange to me
How things could happen in this way
 And expected, too, at three.

DONATED FLOWERS.

While 'neath the flowers, sadly wandering,
 With thoughts of days gone by,
I saw the birds around me squandering,
 Soaring toward the sky.
The gayest of all, a mocking bird,
 Singing his tuneful lay;
The singer, the sweetest ever heard,
 Cheered me along my way.
He recalled to me the magic spell
 Thrown over me last year;
His voice, like yours, I remember well,
 Did sound so sweet and clear.
Because he sang the same sweet song
 That once I heard you sing;
It made my heart beat loud and strong,
 Echoes my soul did ring.
How long I stood, how many hours,
 I don t remember well;

But this I know, I plucked some flowers,
  And they the tale may tell.
And they to you I do gladly send,
  White and red roses, too ;
Accept them, my bonnie young friend,
  I plucked them all for you.

THE WEATHER.

Today the sun looks down in my face,
  The heavens are dazzling bright ;
The earth drinks up its flood of rays,
  The moon comes out at night,
And all the little stars look down,
  Smiling from overhead,
While the night, in her pearly gown,
  Sits watching by my bed
'Til rosy dawn sets in again
  And gray clouds float o'erhead :
When dawn comes the pattering rain
  And thunder, oh such dread '
Now I put on my over shoes,
  And, much against my will,
I'm forced to cross those muddy sloughs
  And trudge up o'er the hill.
And then a blizzard soon sets in,

And wind and sleet and snow,
And hail with some rain mixed in
    Come pouring down below,
' Til the sunlight thro' the arches
    In splendor lights the earth,
And the spring birds 'neath the shadows
    Begin their songs of mirth.

THE FLOOD.

When all the world did wicked grow,
    God's anger was intense ;
Much more so than ever before,
    Or ever shown us since.

To Noah he said commandingly :
    " Build for me an ark ; "
And Noah (understandingly)
    Did work from dawn till dark.

When the ark was thoroughly done,
    To Noah's honest joy,
The good Lord said : " It is well done ;
    Now, I will the world destroy "

" So take thee, Noah, two of each
    Of everything that's clean ;

And for them, from my furore's reach,
  These walls shall be a screen."

Then came a breeze among the trees,
  A rumbling far away;
The shepherd boy in horror sees
  The sunlight fading 'way.

For, o'er the hills a little spot
  Had mounted upon high;
It was but a tiny spot,
  But spreaded o'er the sky.

It chased away the sunlight,
  And blotted out the sun;
And darkness, like eternal night,
  With the tempest had begun.

The eagle 'bove the mountain topped,
  And mounted into the sky:
The little birds in terror stopped
  And whispered: "Danger nigh!"

The cattle of a thousand hills
  Came scampering o'er the plain,
Leaping brooks and silvery rills,
  Rushing from the rain.

They saw sitting upon the hill,
  The ark of gopher wood;
Made by Noah of God's own will,
  To shelter all the good.

Into the ark in terror fled
  Every living thing,
Just as to Noah had been said
  By heaven's only King;

Went two of each and every kind
  Of living creatures in;
But wicked man was left behind
  To perish for his sin.

So then took Noah his three sons
  And all their family in;
But wicked people said, "he jests,"
  And kept on in their sin.

Then Noah prepared to embark,
  On waters not yet seen;
" Oh, man!" he cried, " Fly to the Ark!"
  But man was too unclean;

And so kept on in wickedness
  ' Til God himself revealed
To them in their selfishness,
  That he their fate had sealed.

For fiercer grew the howling wind
    And darker grew the sky,
While lofty oaks did nimbly bend
    And lightning flashed on high.

Then came a burst of thunder wild,
    A shock—such bursting bombs!
They frightened nature's only child
    And echoed 'mong the tombs.

Then a silence—such a hush
    Mortals had never known,
And then a bolt as if to crush
    The hardest mountain stone.

The heavens, they, in anger still,
    Wore one furious frown;
O'er ev'ry hill and vale there fell
    The rain in torrents down.

A raging storm on sea and land,
    And darkness coming on,
Before which mortal dared not stand
    And day could never dawn.

When God's relentless anger fell,
    The people, sore, alarmed,

Thought all of earth, and even hell,
    Might fear such dreaded storm.

O'er all the heights, and ev'ry plain,
    O'er ev'ry hill and vale,
The waters raged, like on the main,
    And fiercer blew the gale.

It raged in furore over earth,
    Crept up the mountain's side;
Ten thousand children, just from birth,
    Were swept on with the tide.

" No mercy for the dying child!
    No ears to heed its cry!"
Were heard to say the waters wild,
    "Mortality must die!"

Man climbed up the tallest tree,
    But that would never do;
" Ha, ha, ha!" laughed the gaping sea,
    " I'm coming up there, too."

Then up the mountain, all defiled,
    He fled to nature's towers,
But, " No, no!" cried the thunders wild,
    "The mountains, they are ours."

But up the mountain on he sped
  Though punishment was due,
And, just for spite, the mad waves said :
  " We're coming up there, too."

And so, hemmed in on ev'ry side,
  He uttered screams of fear;
The echoes rang out far and wide,
  But God refused to hear.

The greedy waves crept o'er his head,
  And heeded not his plea,
But strangled him 'till he was dead,
  Then buried him in the sea.

And then, suddenly thro' the sky
  The sunlight faintly burst ;
A rainbow loomed out on high
  That said, " this ends the curse."

The clouds all quickly passed away,
  The sunbeams lit the sky,
' Twas near the hundred and fiftieth day
  When the waters said good-bye.

Again with furore o'er the lea
  And back towards the West,
They hasten back into the sea
  Where they now calmly rest.

And the Ark, with it precious freight,
  Mid calm and all of that,
Landed, so the Hebrews state,
  Upon Mount Ararat.

Eight persons, only, left the Ark
  And marched across the plain,
Forever aft' in ages dark
  To people the world again.

KAY PULLIAM'S GIN.

TO THE PULLIAM CHILDREN.

NOTE.—One spring evening, while sitting
at my window, near Rossville, Fayette
County, Tennessee, I heard the cry, "fire!
fire!" I rushed to the scene of horror, to
find it the farm gin which belonged to a
farmer by the name of Pulliam. I eagerly
watched the flames as they rose up in
splendor against the vernal skies, and I saw
the old house sink into a mass of ashes. So
touched was I with that scene of mingled
beauty and horror, that I drew from my
pocket a pencil and tablet, and wrote a

poem, which I dedicated to the farmer's
children.—March, 1889.

Hum, hum, hum, went the old gin wheel
   Of old Kay Pulliam's gin.
Zoo, zoo, zoo, through the old sage field
   Loud blew the cutting wind.

But, as the wind blew cold and raw
   Straight through Kay Pulliam's gin,
Gayly sang Mr. Jackson Warr,
   And raked the cotton in.

While he sang as a gay skylark
   A stifling smoke arose.
His eyes caught the glittering spark,
   And his heart within froze.

He called to the driver, ho! ho!
   As would his great grand sire,
Then leaping to the ground below,
   Screamed out—" fire! fire ' fire!"

But onward blew the cutting wind
   Straight through the old dry frame,
A mighty crackling rose within,
   And higher leaped the flame.

And the cows left their pasture feed
  To watch the flames ascend,
But when they smelled the cotton-seed
  They seemed to comprehend.

But fiercer grew the seething flame,
  Of it will memory tell,
How cranky grew the old dry frame,
  At last the old house fell.

Thus ceased the humming of the wheel
  Of old Kay Pulliam's gin,
But zoo, zoo, through the old sage field
  Still blows the cutting wind.

SCHOOL LIFE ENDED.

TO THE CLASS OF 1890.

At last! at the terminus
  Of normal training's day;
But seven if you count us,
  Yet ask what you may.

We rest here but a second;
  Sweet is a moment's rest :

So soon we shall be beckoned
  Onward at God's request.

The waters still are flowing
  Within their murmuring rills ;
The harvest fields are glowing
  Along the sloping hills.

Let's get our sycles ready
  Before the autumn rain,
With hands both firm and steady,
  Reap in the golden grain.

But hark ' we're at the ocean—
  The ocean deep and wide :
We hear its surging billows,
  We see its swelling tide.

And should we launch our vessel
  Upon this stormy sea,
What damage could there happen
  To seven as true as we ?

Tho' on the stormy ocean
  We'd meet with endless strife :
But due us is a portion
  Of trouble thro this life.

So let's be like the seven,
  " The seven peas in a pod,"
That grew beneath the heaven
  For the glory of their God.

But when our " pod " is open
  And the winds our union sever,
Who'll go into the desert
  And the starving birds deliver?

Who'll leap up to the attic
  And thro' the window peep,
To cheer the poor, afflicted,
  And watch them in their sleep?

Who'll go out on the hillside
  Where oft' the shepherds sleep,
And spread your branches wide
  To feed the hungry sheep?

For here our school life ends:
  We dare not try to shirk;
But say " farewell, dear friends,"
  And hie upon our work.

We'll be a happy seven
  Where'er our feet have trod,
And live beneath the heaven
  For the glory of our God.

Tho' with the tempest shifting,
  Or while the sunbeams dart,
With pearly clouds we re drifting
  Farther and farther apart;

Yet we shall be a seven,
  On land or on the main;
Our compass points to heaven,
  And there we'll meet again.

THE FUNNY MAN.

The funniest man I ever saw
  I'll tell you this, you see,
He is about the size of pa,
  And lives with Kitt McCree.

He goes to Macon, gets his drink,
  And then gets on a spree,
But when its off—how strange to think,
  Comes back to Kitt McCree.

He takes his beer and whisky straight,
  Jolly as he can be.
His name to you I will not state—
  He lives with Kitt McCree.

One day while whittling with his knife
   The bark from off a tree,
" Duch," said he to his hearty wife,
   "Just leave old Kitt McCree."

So off he moved to neighbor's house,
   To live with him, you see,
But, before three weeks were quite out,
   Went back to Kitt McCree.

And there he is until this day,
   Jolly as he can be ;
And there he'll be until he's gray
   With same old Kitt McCree.

KING AUTUMN.

Autumn one September day
   With but a golden wand
Came to this country (people say)
   From a strange, foreign land.

He found the earth enrobed in green,
   With flowered belts around,
A skirt of nature's grandest scene
   In tucks of grandeur bound.

He thought her queenly in her form,
  But just one thing alack,
A golden belt, a chain and charm,
  And brownish-colored sack.

And so he touched her queenly hand;
  And trees that graced her crown
Did waver 'neath his magic wand
  Till came a shower down.

He moved among the leafy tents
  Till colors varied came,
And till bouquets of golden tints
  Were given earth his dame.

Then he smiled upon the flowers,
  Which blushed and drooped the head :
And stepping out from the bowers,
  In frigid tones he said :

" I, the great king of all the land,
  Know nothing of mother ;
But early left my native land
  To dwell in another.

The earth at once shall change her robe
  From green to brilliant brown,
And every creature on the globe
  Shall recognize her crown."

He placed his hands upon the leaves
　　Which soon their verdure lost ;
And blew his breath among the eaves
　　And left a coat of frost.

Then we insects and little elves
　　Did vanish as of gold,
And men threw cloaks around themselves
　　Because 'twas getting cold.

And every year since that day,
　　When earth puts on her brown,
All of the wise pull off their gay
　　To recognize her crown.

A FADED FLOWER.

TO " MAGNETTA."

NOTE.—This flower was left by a member of the senior class of 1889 in a Latin reader, in the Normal Institute, LeMoyne, and remained there till found by the class of next year, whence sprang this poem :

O, beautiful, lovely flower,
　　(Between the pages pressed)
Once thou decked a graceful bower,
　　And often was caressed ;

Until a maiden came one day
    To admire their velvet crest,
And plucked thee, took thee far away
    Upon her heaving breast.

She brought thee to this study-room,
    Far from your shady nook,
Between these pages sealed thy doom,
    And kept thee in this book.

She wrote above thee an epitaph,
    Beneath thee something better ;
Across thy other verdant half
    She wrote her name—Magnetta.

She was so pleased with all thy charms,
    With all thy grace and style,
She often clasped thee in her arms,
    Caressed thee with a smile.

She put thee in this self-same place,
    She read this self-same book :
To her you added queenly grace,
    And thee she ne'er forsook.

She was a girl of simple grace :
    Angelic sweetness not amiss,
So often, too, in her embrace,
    Didst thou receive a loving kiss.

But summer time came on at last,
    Commencement day came, too:
She greeted thee her very last,
    And bade thee an adieu.

She left thee a fading flower,
    A treasure more than dear;
But one day 'mid autumn's shower
    We came and found thee here.

We greeted thee for her namesake,
    And let many tear-drops start:
For thee no ruby would we take,
    Yet so soon we, too, must part.

We'll pardon her if she was cruel
    To break thee from thy tree;
Because to us all a jewel,
    Much treasured, you shall be.

So with this ribbon we'll bind you
    And leave you in this book,
So some other class may find you
    And for your hist'ry look.

And now we will part forever:
    The winds some day may tell
That we've forgotten thee never,
    So farewell, dear! farewell!

FATE.

I met her in the country
    When the sun was low,
And the sky was radiant
    With an amber glow.

We played croquet together
    On the school-yard ground,
Till fell the twilight shadows
    And the night came round.

"Good-night, sir!" said she softly,
    As she walked away;
"We'll meet again to-morrow,
    If fine be the day."

Again next day I met her
    In the early morn,
When heard was but the ringing
    Of the hunter's horn.

With me she went afishing,
    Tho' nothing was caught;
I wondered if I loved her.
    Would it come to naught?

We went to church together,
  And she sang a song ;
I dreamed about the singing
  All the night live-long.

I then knew that I loved her,
  And did not repine,
Because that she was promised
  And never could be mine.

But love I will forever,
  Till we meet above ;
For death can never sever
  Bonds of sacred love.

The heaven bells will ring it
  In their merry chimes—
" I love her !"—and be echoed
  Back a thousand times.

The angels all will sing it
  In their melody,
That I will love her ever
  Thro' eternity.

THE KIND REPLY

A Christian man one summer's day
    With care his books perusing,
Was smiling in a pleasant way
    As something seemed amusing.

An open letter in his hand
    Thro' which a friend was pleading,
She who was his dearest friend,
    Her words he had been reading.

When suddenly the door flew wide,
    A stalwart friend came in,
And stepping to the Christian's side
    This story did begin—

" That girl whom oft you call your friend
    Has used you as a tool,
Tho' innocent does she pretend,
    Yet plays you for the fool. "

"Oh, no!" said he, " It all I see
    And fully understand,
That barrier 'twixt her and me
    You wish to take your stand. "

" Oh, no, sir ! " said the stalwart friend,
 " It is a true old tale,
And upon it you may depend,
 Deceit is a female.

Did you not to Stanovilla
 One lovely summer's day,
With your lone red umbrella
 A friendly visit pay?

And when you had departed
 Back forty miles to roam,
She a wicked letter started
 Out on its mission home?

To a girlish friend she stated—
 ' These words I gladly send ;
The question's being debated,
 If not the world's on end.

This day there came to see me,
 My memory makes no slips,
A young man, a perfect beauty,
 With great big liver lips. '

You see I am not a barrier
 Betwixt yourself and friend ;
That girl will prove a terror
 And bite you in the end. "

Then stepped he out thro' the door
    Without a sense of wrong ;
The Christian sank upon the floor
    In thought the day live-long,

At length he rose and with a frown,
    Insulted as he thought,
With pen and ink did he sit down
    And wrote what he ought not.

Said he: "If you in this persist
    Friendship sure must sever,
And then our long-loved friendship end
    Forever and forever. "

He sent the letter on its way
    And tears came to his eye,
But ere the close of that same day
    There came the kind reply—

" Dear sir, you have insulted me,
    But I forgive you this,
For, sorry, sorry you will be
    Ere the dew the grass doth kiss.

And as for welcome at my home,
    I give it to you freely.
And will be glad whene'er you come
    If you believe it really.

But to recall your friendship, sir,
    Such can ne'er be in you,
For if you are a Christian, sir,
    Friendship must continue.

And thus you will some future day,
    When passion you forsake,
Consider things the other way
    And see your own mistake. "

The Christian did, and strange to say,
    Became a wiser man,
And knows that nothing e'en this day
    Can do what kindness can.

And now he teaches ev'ry born
    How anger to defy;
Not by hot words and mocking scorn,
    But with a kind reply.

CHRISTMAS BELLS.

Chime on, O, Christmas bells, chime on !
     As once thou didst of yore,
When broke the stillness of the morn
     With the echoes you bore.
"Peace on earth, good will to men,"
     Is what your echoes told,
And that the angels even then,
     Were playing harps of gold.

Chime on, O, Christmas bells, chime on !
     Amuse the babe new-born,
And with thy peals and welcome sound
     Cheer up the rosy morn ;
And bring into my aching heart
     That Christ of long ago,
That he some blessings may impart,
     I ne'er have felt before.

Chime on, O, Christmas bells, chime on !
     I love thy welcome sound :
Forgive, O Lord, what I have done
     In sin the whole year round.
Those angry words I spoke to friends
     Torment me even yet ;

Help me, O Lord, to make amends,
    And then let me forget.

Chime on, O, Christmas bells, chime on!
    Unite the hearts of friends;
Bring back that joy that once our own
    And happiness it tends:
And when the old year makes its halt,
    Do let us then and there
Lay off our sins and evr'y fault,
    New life begin with prayer.

THANATOS.

O'er nature's extended field
    I am a tyrant king;
Where I my giant sceptre wield,
    No life can ever spring.
E'en the flower, when I walk
    O'er earth with kingly tread,
If by chance I touch its stalk
    It at my feet falls dead.

I chase the birds of the wood
    And kill them just for fun;
They hide, but they never could
    My presence ever shun.

I break up the squirrel's den,
  Their happiness destroy ;
And I the fleet reindeer then
  Into my arms decoy.

I kiss the leaves on the trees,
  And never greived am I
When their verdant beauty flees.
  And nature seems to die ;
For life it is that I haunt,
  In air, on land or sea ;
And funer'l songs I chant—
  " Farewell mortality ! "

Man I shall forever hate.
  (Between us but a pace),
For since Adam's lost estate
  I'm ever on his chase.
I murder his babe—poor child '—
  E'en on its mother's breast ;
Nor heed I screams pleading wild
  Nor grant his vain request ;
But with the babe off I run,
  Making my mission brief,
Looking backward just for fun
  And smiling at his grief.

I visit the sick man's bed,
  And to him I say "Die!"
A moment more and he's dead,
  Such a monster am I.
My strength can ne'er tell its own,
  For space will ne'er give room;
I forced the God from his throne
  And shut him in the tomb.

I the verdant fields disrobe,
  I conquer all the brave;
The air, the sea, e'en the globe
  I make as one great grave.
Over earth on ev'ry hill
  I blow my pois'nous breath,
And write on every house sill
  And ev'ry doorpost—Death.

PROSE EDITION.

SINK, SANK AND SUNK.

Once I had the pleasure of attending an entertainment in a Western metropolis. While there I met a young lady, who introduced herself as Miss Sink, and then proceeded to chat away as familiarly as though we had been friends all of our lives.

O, she knew that I was a young man of first society She was so glad that I had been invited, and wished that I would visit her before leaving the city. Then she sighed, and asked me to take her up to the cafe.

Of course I could not refuse, and, offering her my arm, we strolled out into the moonlight and up to the cafe. I told her that I had forgotten my pocket-book, and had only fifty cents with me (but the truth was that I had only fifty cents in the world,

and owed already a wash bill of ten dollars,
but I kept silent.) We entered the cafe,
and she ordered oysters and cream until my
bill amounted to a dollar.

I got the manager to credit me, promis-
ing to pay him next day. She sighed again,
and called me dear, and said she wanted to
go home in a hack, and I, like a fool, rented
one on a six-hour credit, and carried her
home.

At the door she left me, without saying
good night.

Next day I met her, and addressed her as
Miss Sink, but she replied that her name
was Sank, and that she had no inclination
whatever to speak to strangers on the street,
and so passed on.

When next I met her she smiled sweetly,
and addressed me as "Sunk." I caught
the twinkle of her laughing eyes and knew
that why she called herself "Sink" at our
first meeting was because she meant to sink
me in debt. And when she sank the cream
and oysters down her gullet, or sank back
in a soft cushioned hack at my expense, she
could afford to call herself "Sank." Thus
I turned out to be Mr. "Sunk."

Since then I have not met Miss Sink, but whenever I see a girl too familiar with a lad at first sight methinks that she is certainly Miss Sink, or some very close relation. If I see a girl give a lad a public insult, and turn up her nose and walk away without cause, I know that she is a Miss "Sank."

And, if I see a young lady who will not go out with a young man unless he takes a hack for her, or can not pass a candy shop or cafe without stopping to make a purchase, methinks she must be Miss Sink or her sister. But when I see a young man forsaken by the ladies, and laughed at on the highways, methinks his name is "Sunk."

And whenever I see a merchant over-anxious for someone to take shares with him in business, I feel that he is Miss Sink's papa, and the man who goes in with him will turn out to be Mr. "Sunk."

Or, when I see a man too anxious for public office, methinks him a man who will sink his paws into the public treasury if he gets a chance, and, with the money sank deep into his pockets, will flee to Canada; and, of course, the treasury would be "Sunk."

JUDGE SPARROW'S COURT.

One spring, while walking on the com.
mons, my attention was attracted by two
small humming-birds that were perched on
the back of an old seat, and seemed deeply
interested in something on the ground
below.

I approached within a yard of them, but
they seemed too deeply interested to be
aware of my presence.

Just then a strange chattering noise from
the ground near them made me look sharply
in that direction, and I saw what I supposed
to be all the insects of the world collected
in that quarter.

Drawing near I saw monopeds, bipeds,
tripeds, quadrupeds, centipeds, millepeds,
cephalapeds, and all other kinds of peds;
and each seemed equally interested in something that was taking place in the centre of
the circle.

I cast a glance in that direction and saw a
giant spider pushing up his sleeves and preparing to fight a little black ant no larger
than his great toe. The ant seemed very

unwilling to fight one so much larger than he; but a busy, fuss-making fly, took the ring and urged on the fight.

"Go on him, I tell you. If he is bigger than you, that is nothing, for you can whip him any way."

Then he would run behind the spider and push him forward, saying:

"Go on him' for you can whip that little ant, for I can myself." And then he would throw the ant forward and cry: "Take him, I tell you, take him'" Then all the insects began to yell, and an old dirt-dobber clapped his hands and shouted so that I thought he would twist himself in two. Then the spider made a mark and forbade the ant to cross it.

The ant, who by this time had become enraged, forbade the spider to cross his own mark. In a twinkling the spider was over the mark and upon the ant. Then the fight began. Now the spider, then the ant. Over and under, under and over, till the insects huddled together and took bets on the fight.

"I'll bet on the ant," said the dirt-dobber.

"I'll bet on the spider," said the snail.

"And I, too," said the wasp.

"I'll bet on the ant," said the worm.

"And I on the spider," said the beetle.

"Well," said daddy long-legs, "I'll take bets on them both, and surely one of them will win."

And so the bets went around and the humming-birds were to hold the stakes. The fly in the meanwhile was urging on the fight, and now and then would cry, "I told you so! Don't that little man kick! I knew that he would whip the spider, but I only wanted to see the fight; ha, ha, ha; hurrah for the ant!"

Just then the spider, enraged because he could not whip the ant, turned upon the fly and gave him a mortal wound in his side with his dagger. Thus fell the fly that urged on the fight. The other insects began to yell and to turn about for the stake-holders, but the humming-birds had flown and no trace of them could be found. Then an all-round fight was engaged in by the bettors, while the little ant slipped out and told police sparrow that an insurrection had been raised on the commons. And he went down and arrested the rioters and took

them before Judge Sparrow's court   I fol-
lowed them to the court and found a half-
dozen half-starved English sparrows reading
the Code of England, and who called themselves lawyers, while Judge Sparrow re-
clined in a great arm chair and looked over
his spectacles at the criminals.

After a jury had been summoned the
spider was brought forward under a charge
of murder, but he turned State's evidence
against the crowd that urged on the fight.
Then the jurors retired to render their verdict.   They soon returned with a verdict—
" Guilty of complicated crime."

Then the attorney went to the library and
brought out a large book which he called
" Treaty on Complications, " and read to
the judge thus :   " If any bug or insect of any
nationality or country be found guilty of
complicated crime, and said bug or insect
be under the sparrow government at the
time when the crime is committed, it shall
be turned over to the sparrow court and devoured by the lawyers "

These words had scarcely fallen from the
attorney's lips when the half-starved lawyers leaped over the table and began to d e

vour the poor insects, while the judge, thinking that if he tarried none would be left for himself, turned over his chair, broke his spectacles and joined in the feast with much avidity.

I left the court, fully assured that when I see a crowd of boys or men urging others to fight there will be a complicated crime committed.

And when one is too easily persuaded to have a law suit over what he might settle peaceably, it is sure to turn out to be a com. plicated affair, and the complainant turned over to Judge Sparrow's court to be devoured by some lawyer.

TOM STITZLEWEED.

Once there lived in the neighborhood of Memphis a youth by the name of Tom. His parents were of a good family and determined to raise little Tom to some great prominence if it were possible to do so. Forthwith they exhausted all their little savings to provide Tom with books and paper, such as suited best. He learned rapidly, and was much carried away with the history of great men, so much so that he determined himself to become one of them. But which would he be?

The question puzzled him very much, for he found his little head quite overrun with ideas.

At last he determined to learn French and become a consul for his country. No sooner decided than commenced. He learned French without the aid of a teacher and with astonishing rapidity. In fact, within a few years he was able to read French newspapers with as much ease as a little boy can rob a swallows nest. This accomplished, he thought himself fit for office, and at once

began to discuss the name that he would
assume, for all great men must have great
names, and he decided upon "Stitzleweed,"
which he thought as foreign as harmonious.
This done, he sat down and wrote a letter
to the President, thus :—

"Foret Coline, Jan. 1st, 19th Century.
"*Dear Sir :*—I demand your highness to
take the lofty ascension to the extent of
building a new fleet to send my unequaled
excellence as consul to France. Demands
rapid movement on the part of your highness. I remain,   Very Respectable,
"Sir Thomas Stitzleweed,
"Bachelor of all Trades."

When this was received the President was
so astonished that for a long time he knew
not what to do, and for all I know he is astonished yet. However, Tom did not seem
much disappointed when he received no
answer from his highness, and only said :
"Just what I expected ; another one of
those low-bred, uneducated fellows, who
can't read good writing when he gets it. I
don't want to be consul, anyway ; it's too
low a station for me ; besides I'm born for
a New York merchant."

He thought sure that he could make such a successful merchant that all the world would be astonished at his fame; so at once he set to work to decide upon his line of business. He finally decided to deal in lamps, wicks and watch cords; but in order to carry out his plans it was necessary to have a machine; therefore he resorted at once to his library to look over some circulars of the most noted firms in New York.

At last he saw an advertisement of the Glove Novelty Co. of a toy Knitting Machine. "This," said he, "is the very thing, and I'll send for it at once." So saying he sent a post-haste message to the company, and then hurried to tell his sweetheart of his plans. "You are as crazy as a bed bug," said she; "don't tell me anything about it." "Just wait till I tell you something about it, won't you?" said Tom. "Why, my dear, it will knit at least 1,000 wicks per second, and I will sell them at five for a nickel and realize no less than $200 per second, you see, and you will wear imported silks and diamond crowns and live in a castle of pure gold, and be called Mrs. Lady Stitzleweed, Batcheloress of all trades."

Elated at this. she consented to give the work a trial, and Tom went home happier than ever.

In a few days the machine came.   It was a small spool with four pins driven in the end, and a little hole in the middle about large enough for a bedbug to crawl through.

Tom scrutinized it closely, and then began hunting some directions how to use it, and finding none, exclaimed, "Ah! they knew I was an inventor, and that's why they didn't send me any of their nonsense. Well, I am going to invent a plan for using it;" and he tugged away and tugged away, from rosy morn till close of day, and yet no means did he invent for the use of his machine.   Month after month passed till six months had gone and yet Tom had invented no means for the use of his machine.

At last he carried it to his sweetheart to ask her aid in making it knit.   She was disgusted with the machine and thought her chance for a gold palace very poor, but she said nothing, and set to work with it, and in a few minutes had knitted a nice cord.

"Sarah," exclaimed Tom, "I knew that your head was level, and you will be the making of me yet." Thus saying, he repaired to his own house to commence his business. An old dilapidated stable was chosen for the storehouse, and the trough was taken for his work-bench. This done, he was ready to commence.

He hung out a long sign, which read thus :

SIR THOMAS STITZLEWEED, A. B. T.

Wholesale Dealer in

LAMPWICKS AND WATCHCORDS.

He set to work, thinking meanwhile that in a few moments he would see his store house over-run with lampwicks and cord, but he toiled away and fumed and raged but could not increase the work of his machine. Six months passed again and Christmas came and Sarah wanted a Christmas present but poor Tom had exhausted all his money with what he called—"that confounded machine," and had knitted but three wicks which he could not sell or even give away if he tried.

The passers-by laughed him to scorn and he became miserable. At last he decided

to run it by steam; therefore he dug a large
hole in the ground, filled it with powder,
charged the fuse with cotton which he
lighted, and placing the machine over the
hole, waited for consequent action. Alas
for poor Tom! His boiler exploded and
carried his machine like lightning towards
the moon, and it never came down again;
and for all I know it is up there still, knitting lamp-wicks for the man in the moon.
He at once concluded that he was not born
for such a low station as a merhant and
decided at once to become a stenographer
and telegraph operator. He thought that
sure he would be successful in that; and at
once began the study. He provided himself with a " MORSE-SNAPPER " with
which he had but small success, and on the
part of stenography, he learned nothing:
but he thought himself the wisest man in the
world in that profession.

One day he decided to try his new
"snapper" on the public telegraph line. No
sooner decided than done. Now the snapper was only a piece of thin iron in shape
of a frog, but Tom thought it wonderful and
tried to attach it to the "main line." To do

this he had to throw it upward of about fifty feet. This he did time after time but each time it came to the ground again, till at last it hung among the wires and Tom could not get it down again, and he climbed and chunked and threw sticks against the wires but the "snapper" hung there apparently unconscious of Tom's threats until he grew tired and went home. And for all I know it is still hanging there sending dispatches to Washington. But our young man (for such he was) was not disposed to give up so easily, and said : " It was a cheap machine and I shall get a better;" and he did. He secured a perfect machine with full set of batteries and repaired to one of the city schools of which he was a pupil and obtained permission from the Professor, to stretch his telegraph line from the window of the school to an outer house in the school yard.

This done he entered an alliance with a friend who was to bear half the expense; and in a few days a sign went up bearing these illustrious names —

> ## CRANKYBOY & STITZLEWEED.
> ### Telegraphers and Stenographers.

Then Tom repaired to his seat at the window and turning on the electricity, would send message after message to his friend in the outer house; not knowing what he himself was doing, he wondered that if his friend knew: therefore he would rush to the window and bawl out across the yard "Say partner did you understand that? I wrote S-a-m!"

Of course "Crankyboy" understood it after he was told, and he told Tom so. Then he would retire to his seat for a few minutes, and would soon come running to the door crying at the top of his voice, "Say, pards! did you understand that? I wrote–T-o-m;" and Tom would say yes, he understood it perfectly.

But, unfortunate for Tom, just as he hoped for success the monopoly fell through and they were obliged to abandon their work.

Sarah became so much disgusted at her sweetheart s failure that she kicked him and married a well to do farmer and moved out of the country This almost ran Tom crazy but he tried to bear with it, saying—"It's sad but I can't help it, and I should have known that I could never be a successful stenographer when my talent runs only in the line of art." He spoke truthfully for he had a wonderful talent in that line, but his paintings never amounted to much. He sallied forth out into the great wide world till he found another partner as equally given to building air castles as he. This new friend was known by the name of Tom Fizzleton and was as big a simpleton as Stitzleweed, so they entered an alliance; Fizzleton as an inventor and Stitzleweed as an artist. After providing themselves with necessary meterials and Stitzleweed with his lensless "Camera," they were ready for business and opened up on one of the prominent streets of the city with this sign hanging from the door :

STITZLEWEED, FIZZLETON & CO.
Artists & Inventors.

In a few days a country gentleman, seeing the sign, stopped to have his picture taken. "Bully for me!" said Stitzleweed, (to himself) "I shall have success right away." (Then, addressing the stranger), " Have a seat, sir! What kind of a picture would you like, side view or full view ?— though I know what kind will suit you best. Sway your head back! Now, sir! Tuck your feet up, they might spoil a good picture. Now, sir! All ready, here she goes." And he produced an excellent picture of the ceiling and a hole through which the stove pipe use to be, but no sign of the stranger. " Not a very good picture sir, but its all your fault because you were not elevated high enough. This machine will take an excellent picture of the man in the moon, Suppose that next time, sir, you come through the back door of the moon and take your seat on the front banisters; then I will be able to take a more perfect picture—How much do I charge you? O, nothing for the picture sir, only a dollar for my trouble—Good day!" He retired to his private office. In a few moments there came another knock at the door. "My gracious, shouted he, I'll be worked to death in one day!—Come in!—Be seated! Do you want a picture taken, sir? Well, climb up on the step-ladder there, so that you may be high enough—Now, sir—All right—Here she goes'" And he produced a picture of the man's feet. "Not a good picture, sir; but not my fault—See? Your feet are too large. They hide your whole body!—O, the body is there; yes, sir, if you could only get over behind those feet to see it. What do I charge? only two dollars, sir!" "Two dollars!" exclaimed the astonished visitor "Yes. sir; why that is cheap for those two big feet Thank you, sir—Good day' Meanwhile Fizzleton was busy in his office inventing rubber stamps and patent door-bells. 'Come in'" said he as some one knocked at the door In a few moments a visitor entered and asked to see some of his inventions. "With pleas-

ure, sir: here is the ninth wonder of the
world !" (handing him a half-sided rubber
stamp); " I sell those at fifty dollars apiece."
"Fifty dollars !" said the stranger, "why
you ought to be very rich. How many
have you sold ?" " None yet; but I ex-
pect to sell some. Look here !" said he,
(holding up a paper door-bell), " this is the
tenth wonder of the world. Why, sir ! this
is the surest guard against theft and robbery
ever invented. If you hang it on the door
at night and a thief ventures into the house,
it will run all over the place squalling ' thief:
thief! burglar ! robber ! and so on."

"Well, I do declare !" said the stranger,
you ought to send it to Washington and
get it patent righted." "Well," said Fizzleton, " I had not thought of that but I'll
send it up to the President right away.
Much oblige to you, sir. Good day !
And he did send it to the President that
very same day; but he received no reply;
and for all I know, if the President did not
light his pipe with it, it is up there yet.

CHAPTER II.

Next morning the city authorities broke up the firm of STITZLEWEED & FIZZLETON under the charge of "Pretense," and the young men had to resort to other means for making their living. Their ingenuity soon devised a plan and they at once became actors on the stage.

Stitzleweed was to traverse the country giving Concerts and Bible Sceneries while Fizzleton canvassed the city with theatricals and "minstral-plays." Many suns set in the cloudbanks of the west and many moons rose in the heavens to look down with pity upon the two unfortunate Toms, and the thunder-heads in the far away sky wept so bitterly that tears fell like showers of rain, and yet Stitzleweed tugged on in the country, sometimes in mud up to his shins and sometimes abused and disappointed till six months wore away without success, and Fizzleton in the town, who had spent six months in getting up a play called "Esmeralda," in which he was sure of making over forty thousand dollars, had failed to make even forty cents.

This convinced them that they were not
born for stage actors and they decided to
marry before they became too old.   No
sooner decided than courtship commmenced.
They took "Crankyboy" into their employ as
manager of private notes, etc.   This done
they hung out the sign—

STITZLEWEED, FIZZLETON, CRANKYBOY & CO.

Wholesale, Commission and Retail Merchants,

Dealers in

Courtships, Marriages, etc.

Then as Crankyboy was not to go along
with them they decided to have their visit-
ing cards struck thus :—

STITZELWEED & FIZZLETON,

COURTSHIP CHUMS.

This done, they set out together to see a
girl on whom they were both smitten.
They would go and sit for hours looking at
her and playing with the children without
saying a word, then go home thinking that

they had had a big evening, and they would often send valuable presents in such abundance that the girl had to send them back. One evening on meeting her at a public gathering, they wished to see her home and wrote to her :

" Fair Lady :

" Shall we have the blissful felicity of your graceful condecension to the extent of allowing our royal excellence to perambulate in close proximinity to your angelic presence— ma'am ? Yours, S., F. & Co."

To this note they received no reply but they thought it was because they had no buggy ; so they decided next time to carry a buggy Fizzleton had an old horse which was so poor that the people of that vicinity had named him Soap-Sticks because they had been waiting for him to die, that they might make soap out of him. So after borrowing and old buggy from a neighbor, they hitched Soap-sticks to it and led him around to the girl's house. Fizzleton and the girl got into the dilpidated old cart and said, "go along Soap-sticks;" but Soap-sticks could not be bribed and he didn t move a step, so Snizleweed had to walk before him and shake a bundle of fodder at him in order to coax him along. They had not gone many paces before the shay broke through at the bottom and the wheels took a notion to go in different directions and down different streets, while "Soap-Sticks" climbed an elevated yard and began to graze with increasing appetite, leaving Fizzleton and the girl sitting in the mud in the middle of the street, and Stitzleweed standing dumfounded looking on with horror, till a policeman came along and arrested them for a nuisance. The girl swore by the days of earth that she would break the first one's head with the baby crib that darkened her door after that; and thus they parted. Being disgusted at so many failures they dissolved partnership; and the last I heard of them, "Soap-Sticks" had gone with the buzzards on a trip to the moon, Crankyboy had entered an academy for learning, Fizzleton was ranking under the title of 'fessor in an industrial school and Stitzleweed was trying to be a jack-leg preacher, and for all I know he is still preaching to the heathens on the shores of Africa, and may continue preaching till "Soap-Sticks" gets back from the moon.

A BACKWOODS STORY

One day as Uncle Alf Jennings sat in front of my school room busy making baskets for his neighbors, I left the children for a few minutes to themselves to have a pleasant chat with this busy old basket-maker. "Uncle Alf," said I, approaching him. will you tell me a story of your past life?"

The old gentleman looked up with a smile and said slowly. "It will give me great pleasure indeed if you will be seated;" and he twisted a stool around for me to sit on, then laying down his pipe and pushing away his basket began his story in true western style.

"One October's evening as the full moon rose in the East and the stars began to twinkle over head in South Eastern Missouri. I left my home to carry a message to Jasper some ten miles away.

"The route was a perilous one because the country had not been settled and the woods were filled with wild and fierce animals. For this reason I armed myself with a revolver, a bowie and a club and set out on my journery. I was a young man then and could run about as swift as any Texas pony; therefore, I had decided, if I should be attacked, to display my talent as a runner, and, if caught, to fight it out like a man. My path led me across a two-mile stretch of prairie to a dark and dismal heath. I kept a sharp lookout for wolves and was nearly across a two-mile stretch of prairie when suddenly I saw directly before me, in the light of the moon, a lean, lanky creature who was slowly approaching me, but feigned unconsciousness of my approach. I stopped long enough to see what it was— a wolf—then drew my club and waited his approach. On he came within ten feet of me, then raising his head as though he had just known of my presence, rushed at my throat. I received him with a blow from my club which doubled him up in the tall prairie grass, but in a second he was up and, like a flash, he went by me, carrying a large piece of my pantaloons with him; and before I could prepare to strike he came back for another piece. This time I ran after him and dealt him such blows on the shank with my club that he turned with fury upon

me and went again for my throat, but then
I began to display so much skill as a wolf-
fighter that he retired to a little hill and
began a howl for reinforcement. I knew
if I should tarry longer the prairie would
be black with wolves. Not far away I
heard the sound of the hunter's horn and
hastened in that direction. I soon found
the hunter and told him my story. Even
then the wolf could be heard howling
from the hill. After listening to my story
the hunter hastened to give chase to the
wolf. I waited a few minutes to determine
the direction in which the wolf was fleeing.
Wnen I knew he had taken the opposite direction I proceeded to enter the heath. It
was a low woodland, some seven miles in
breadth and thickly covered with under
shrub and branches, while the moon beams,
stealing softly through the tree-tops and
falling upon the shrub-berry bushes, cast
fantastic shadows along my pathway, and
the scream of the night-hawk, the howl of
the wolf, the whoop of the panther or the
cry of the catamount sent daggers of fear
through me. I kept on my course for several miles when I met a cavalcade of pion-

eers, who, after learning where I was going,
declared I would never make it—'for just
across the woods,' said they, 'there is a
panther as large as a Texas pony, and has
been following us for more than three miles.
It has just turned off at the west fork of the
road; but if you think you can make it, go
ahead, and good luck to you.'

"They galloped on, and I hastened forward, keeping a sharp look-out on either
side for the panther.

"Luckily I reached the clearing without
meeting with any encounter, and just a mile
in the distance the glimmering lights of
Jasper burst upon my vision, while just beyond, some hundred yards, full in the light
of the moon, I could see the dwelling house
of a farmer. Inspired with new courage,
and thinking that all danger was now
passed, I walked leisurely along, admiring
the pearls of a shadowy night and watching
the stars swinging in their orbits, leaving behind them the most brilliant arcs of light.
For fully half an hour I amused myself thus
and had gone just twenty yards beyond the
farmer's house when the dogs broke out and
rushed pell-mell toward the road. At first

I thought them to be after me, but on turning around I saw, not twenty yards behind
me an object, which at first I took to be a
colt, but on second sight I recognized it as
a panther. He turned in quick warfare
with the dogs; but I, who never liked war,
did not wait to see who would be the
victors, but turned and fled, hat in hand,
across the clearing towards Jasper. The
faint, glimmering lights in the distance
grew brighter and brighter till now they
seemed to be flying towards me with wonderful rapidity, till I was within twenty
yards of the village store, when the door
flew open and the keeper, in the door, cried
out to me: 'Hasten' for not fifty yards
behind is a panther in hot pursuit.' I put
forth my best efforts in trying to reach the
store, but strength had almost failed me and
the panther was not twenty yards behind
me. I made one leap and fell helpless in
the door. The keeper dragged me in and
shut the door just as the panther leaped
with full force against it; then he went to
the window and fired a fatal shot, striking
the panther in the left eye. There was an
awful cry and growling, and I crept to the

window in time to see him leap some ten
feet into the air, and then, after turning
around and around like a kitten trying to
play with its tail, he set off at full speed towards the clearing, but dropped down dead
in about fifty yards from the store. That
night I slept soundly, and the next morning, in company with the people of Jasper,
we went out to look at the panther. He
was about fifteen feet in length and weighed
six hundred pounds. When the people
heard my story they gave me an applause
and said that my journey through the heath
was a daring one that no young man of that
day would dare undertake alone."

*   *   *   *   *   *   *

When the old gentleman had finished he
resumed his pipe and returned to his work.
I gave him my hand and thanked him ; then
returned to the school-room much interested
in the old man s story.

A MID-OCEAN STORY.

It was in mid-autumn of 1856, that a cruising vessel left New orleans, on a cruising expedition along the cost of the Atlantic. On board of the ship went a colored lad as assistant fireman. This lad, whose name was George Bassad, was a youth of great dexterity besides having a fair knowledge of steam machinery.

Not withstanding that the ship had been examined and declared to be perfectly safe by an old ship-builder, George found fault with the machinery and said it would not do to trust. At this the cruisers laughed and said that they wanted none of his advice. So George said no more and went very reluctantly at his work, always keeping a sharp lookout for accidents.

They sailed out of the gulf at a speed of fourteen knots till they were on the broad and deep Atlantic Then the captain ordered the sails to be lowered and the vessel ploughed smoothly and slowly along the coast of the United States, then set sail for mid-ocean, bound for the South-Sea Islands.

For eight days they sailed under the clear, blue skies of the tropics, and every heart seemed elated with joy and every voice uttered words of cheer. On the ninth day the sails were again lowered and the ship ploughed along in mid-ocean. Everybody wore a smiling face except George, who was carefully inspecting the boiler. While he was thus engaged a covey of small birds, like paraquets, settled upon the rear of the vessel and hid behind the riggings. This was observed by the superstitious captain, who at once went to look at the barometer, and finding that it indicated an approaching tempest, ordered the sails to be hoisted and preparation to be made to outstrip a storm. The riggings were soon in order and the ship moved off at a speed of nine leagues an hour. In a few moments the southern sky was blackened like unto midnight and the ligtning was seen playing along the horizon. It was evident that the storm was pursuing them at a rate less than eight leagues per hour, for soon they had lost sight of the clouds and all seemed calm and sunshine again.

The sun was just setting along the western horizon and casting its golden wand upon the waters, was changing them into fantastic temples and fairy palaces of chrystal gold, while from an eastern window the moon was hanging a shade of pearls when suddenly the captain shouted "fly ahead." This cry brought all hands to the deck, and everybody wished to know the trouble, when suddenly a dark cloud was seen boiling up from the south. It was now evident that the storm was still pursuing them and at a madder rate than before. "George," said the captain, "what do you think of the boiler now?" George only shook his head, for he had been looking for an explosion for more than three weeks. He moved away slowly to the edge of the deck, took up a bucket of water and walked back towards the boiler When within a few feet of the boiler he had a strange foreboding of danger, and as quick as a flash threw himself on the floor. Not a moment too soon, for just then the boiler burst and the whole place was filled with hot and scalding steam. All those standing near when the boiler bursted were instantly killed, except George, who was lying upon the floor and below the steam, still unhurt. When he arose from the floor he found the ship deserted and in a sinking condition, with no one aboard but himself and the mate, who was putting on a life preserver and preparing to jump overboard. "Can you swim?" he asked, as George approached." "No," came the answer, "but I'll find means of escape. Where is the other part of the crew?" "O, they left in the life-boat when the boiler first exlpoded," said the mate; "but we all are lost, see!" and he pointed to a fierce storm raging within a half league of them. George could not swim and he realized his perilous condition, for the waters were even then rolling over the deck of the sinking ship. He grasped a p'ank that was filled with holes at either end and with a sharp knife cut pieces of rope from the mast riggings and made hand and foot holds in the ends of the plank, then catching his feet in the ropes at one end and his hands in the other, tumbled over-board into the dark and raging sea. He sank at first, but soon came to the sur-face, and working his hands and feet in the ropes made the plank dart forward with the rapidity of a racing yacht. The mate swam lightly along beside him. The heavens now wore one furious frown and the lightning played magical tricks in the shape of blaz-ing serpents not five fathoms above the water, while the sea raged and foamed and the mad waves leaped into the clouds and fell back with a deafening roar into the sea. But on sped George and the mate, some-times carried into the clouds and sometimes

buried not less than ten fathoms below the
sea. Several hours passed and then the sea
was calm again and the two men floated
quietly upon the surface of the waters.
"Are you safe, George?" the mate shouted,
as the plank floated near him. "Safe as a
monkey in the cocoanut grove of India,"
said George, apparently at ease upon his
plank.

The stars were now racing along the horizon and the moon smiled serenely down
from her palace of pearls upon the last of
the cruisers, as they drifted together hither
and thither upon the deep bed of the ocean.
Suddenly another object fell upon their visions—a light upon the waters was moving
towards them. Both men speeded forward,
deeply interested in the strange light. At
last George shouted: "It is a schooner and
it is coming toward us; we are safe! thank
God! Oh, heavens' we are safe'"

In a few seconds long streams of light
were cast upon the waters where they were
lying, and then they heard a command on
board to lower the boat, and in a few minutes the dip of oars were heard approaching
them. In a few seconds more they were
hauled into the life-boat and carried into
the ship. Then the captain told how that
he had seen them floating, like chunks, upon
the water, and after discovering that they
were men, ordered the life-boat to be low-

ered ; but when he heard from the two men their story of the sunken ship and their perilous ride over the raging sea, he and all the crew were astonished and set out at once to rescue those who had escaped in the life-boat from the fatal ship.

The schooner sped over the sea at a speed of eighteen knots for more than six hours, but no sign was seen of the little life-boat and its burden of precious freight. At noon the next day the captain gave up the search and set sail towards the north. After eight days rapid sailing the schooner anchored in the port of New Orleans. No news had been received of the lost crew and all agreed that the two picked up by the schooner were the last of the cruisers. They were put under the care of doctors till they were well and able to go to their homes. George Bassad is still alive and quite an old man.

It was from his own lips that I learned this story.

www.ingramcontent.com/pod-product-compliance
Lightning Source LLC
Chambersburg PA
CBHW021135020726
47500CB00003B/1087